The Missing Magic

Read more
UNICORN DIARIES
books!

1. Unicorn Diaries — Bo's Magical New Friend — Rebecca Elliott — SCHOLASTIC

2. Unicorn Diaries — Bo and the Dragon-Pup — Rebecca Elliott — SCHOLASTIC

3. Unicorn Diaries — Bo the Brave — Rebecca Elliott — SCHOLASTIC

4. Unicorn Diaries — The Goblin Princess — Rebecca Elliott — SCHOLASTIC

5. Unicorn Diaries — Bo and the Merbaby — Rebecca Elliott — SCHOLASTIC

6. Unicorn Diaries — Storm on Snowbelle Mountain — Rebecca Elliott — SCHOLASTIC

7. Unicorn Diaries — The Missing Magic — Rebecca Elliott — SCHOLASTIC

8. Unicorn Diaries — Welcome to Sparklegrove — Rebecca Elliott — SCHOLASTIC

Unicorn Diaries

The Missing Magic

Rebecca Elliott

BRANCHES

SCHOLASTIC INC.

For Theo, who has brought magic
into my life in so many ways. XX — R.E.

Special thanks to Clare Wilson
for her contributions to this book.

Library of Congress Cataloging-in-Publication Data

Names: Elliott, Rebecca, author, illustrator.
Title: The missing magic / Rebecca Elliott.
Description: First edition. | New York : Branches/Scholastic Inc., 2022. |
Series: Unicorn diaries ; 7 | Audience: Ages 5–7. | Audience: Grades
K–2. | Summary: Unicorn Bo and friends attend the Big Festival of Magic
hoping to show off their magical skills, but when all the magic goes
missing they must find a way to find and return the magic.
Identifiers: LCCN 2021040213 (print) | LCCN 2021040214 (ebook) | ISBN
9781338745573 (paperback) | ISBN 9781338745580 (hardcover) | ISBN
9781338745597 (ebk) Subjects: CYAC: Unicorns—Fiction. | Magic—Fiction. | Lost and found
possessions—Fiction. | Diaries—Fiction. | LCGFT: Diary fiction.
Classification: LCC PZ7.E45812 Mi 2022 (print) | LCC PZ7.E45812 (ebook) |
DDC [Fic]—dc23 LC record available at https://lccn.loc.gov/2021040213
LC ebook record available at https://lccn.loc.gov/2021040214

ISBN 978-1-338-74558-0 (hardcover) / ISBN 978-1-338-74557-3 (paperback)

10 9 8 7 6 5 4 3 2 1   22 23 24 25 26

Printed in China 62
First edition, September 2022

Edited by Katie Carella
Book design by Marissa Asuncion

Table of Contents

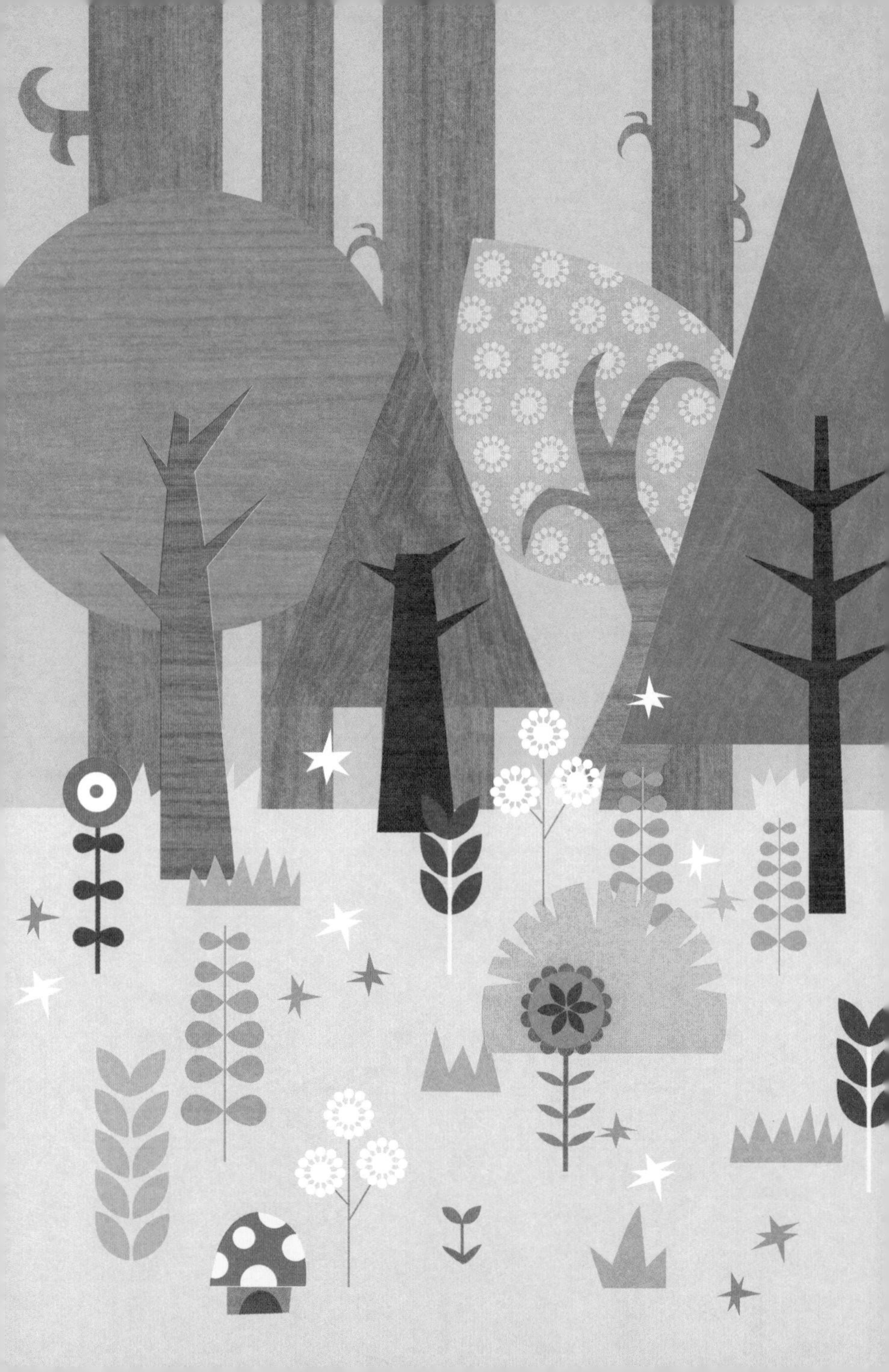

Sunday

Hello, Diary! It's me again — Rainbow Tinseltail. My friends call me Bo.

This is an exciting week because it's when the forest has its Big Festival of Magic! But I will tell you more about that later.

I live in Sparklegrove Forest, a place full of MAGIC!

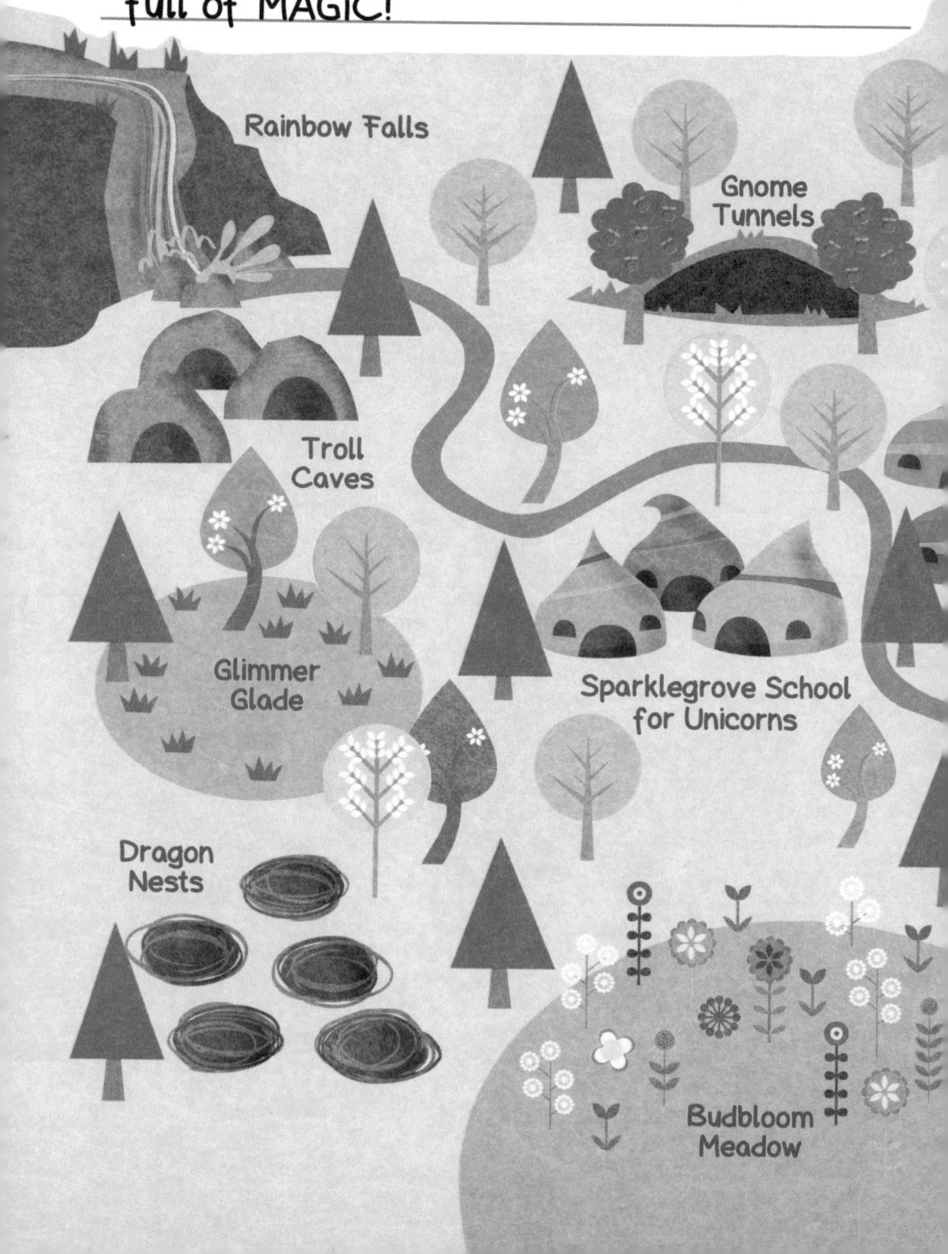
Rainbow Falls
Gnome Tunnels
Troll Caves
Glimmer Glade
Sparklegrove School for Unicorns
Dragon Nests
Budbloom Meadow

Snowbelle Mountain

Unipods

Fairy Village

Goldie's Cave

Twinkleplop Lagoon

Goblin Castle

Lots of magical creatures live here . . .

Like gnomes! Here are four things I know about gnomes:

They live underground.

They are some of the oldest creatures in the forest. (They live for hundreds of years!)

They like to help non-magic creatures.

They love gardening and wearing hats.

Some unicorns wear hats, too! Want to know more about unicorns?

Tail
Swishing it makes our Unicorn Power work. (It's also good for sweeping away cobwebs!)

Rainbow Mane
We can keep stuff in it! (And we hate getting knots in it!)

ACHOO!

Hooves
When we dance, small rainbows shoot out of them!

Nose
When we sneeze, glitter explodes out of it!

Here are more cool **UNIFACTS** for you:

Our horns light up so we can see in the dark.

Instead of being born, unicorns **POP** into the world on really starry nights!

Unicorns have never seen a squirrel!
We don't believe they exist.

When we yawn, colorful musical
notes sparkle around us.

I go to Sparklegrove School for Unicorns (S.S.U.). My friends and I live here, in **UNIPODS**!

We all have different Unicorn Powers. I'm a Wish Unicorn.

I can grant one wish every week!

This is my BEST friend, Sunny Huckleberry. He can turn invisible!

Sunny Huckleberry

Crystal-Clear Unicorn

Here are my other friends, and our teacher.

Nutmeg Silvertips
Flying Unicorn

Scarlett Sugarlumps
Thingamabob Unicorn

Jed Glitterock
Weather Unicorn

Monty Dumpling
Size-Changer Unicorn

Piper Forestine
Healer Unicorn

Mr. Rumptwinkle
our teacher
Shape-Shifter Unicorn

We study **TWINKLE-TASTIC** subjects at S.S.U., like:

SWIMMING

COLORFUL COOKERY

MAGICAL
LANGUAGES

UNIPOD
BUILDING AND
REPAIR

We also practice sewing, because we each have a special patch blanket. Every week, we try to do something new to earn a patch. We sew patches on here to keep track of everything we've learned!

I can't wait to hear what patch we're working toward this week! Good night, Diary!

2

Use Your Magic!

At breakfast, we were all getting excited for the Big Festival of Magic.

I can't believe it's this Saturday!

Then I noticed
Sunny looked a bit
confused.

I'd forgotten that Sunny appeared only a few months ago! So this will be his first festival.

Everyone, let's tell Sunny more about the Big Festival of Magic.

It's a celebration where creatures use their magic to entertain everyone.

The goblin queen holds the festival on Budbloom Meadow.

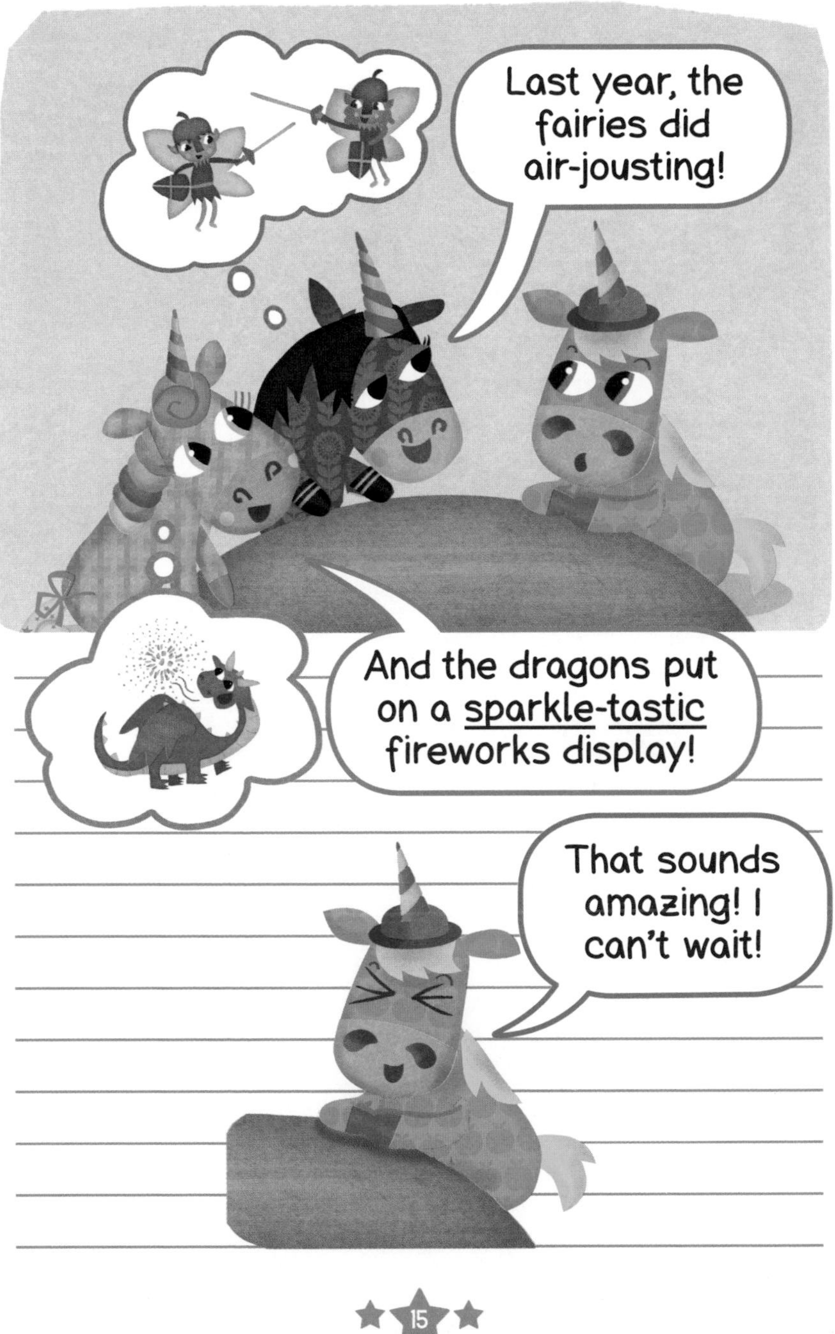
Last year, the fairies did air-jousting!
And the dragons put on a sparkle-tastic fireworks display!
That sounds amazing! I can't wait!

Then we trotted into our classroom, and Mr. Rumptwinkle told us something surprising.

This year's festival will be better than ever, because you get to show off your magical skills, too!

We do?!

Can you believe it, Diary? We actually get to take part this year! And guess what Mr. Rumptwinkle told us next . . .

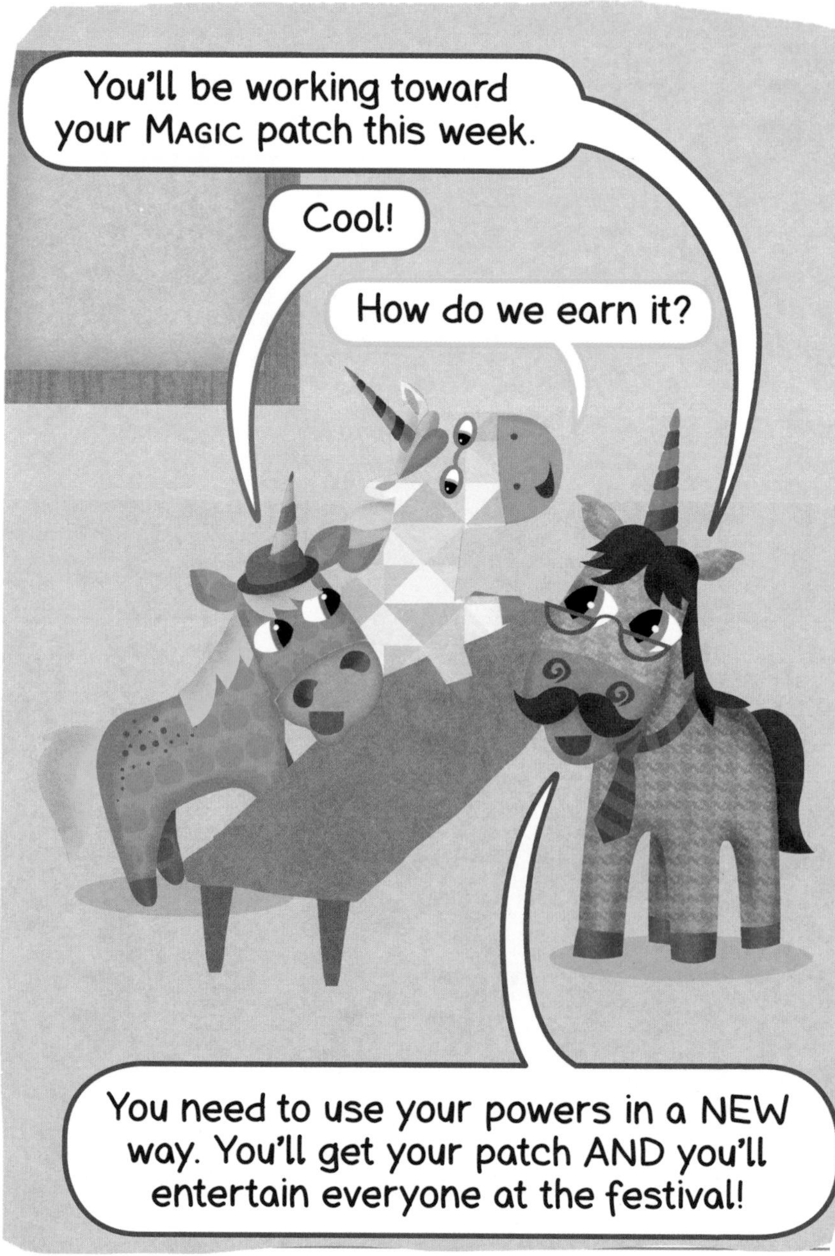

You'll be working toward your MAGIC patch this week.
Cool!
How do we earn it?
You need to use your powers in a NEW way. You'll get your patch AND you'll entertain everyone at the festival!

We all thought hard about different ways to use our powers.

I'm going to learn to fly somersaults!

I'm going to magic a GIANT cake out of my mane! I've only managed a cupcake so far.

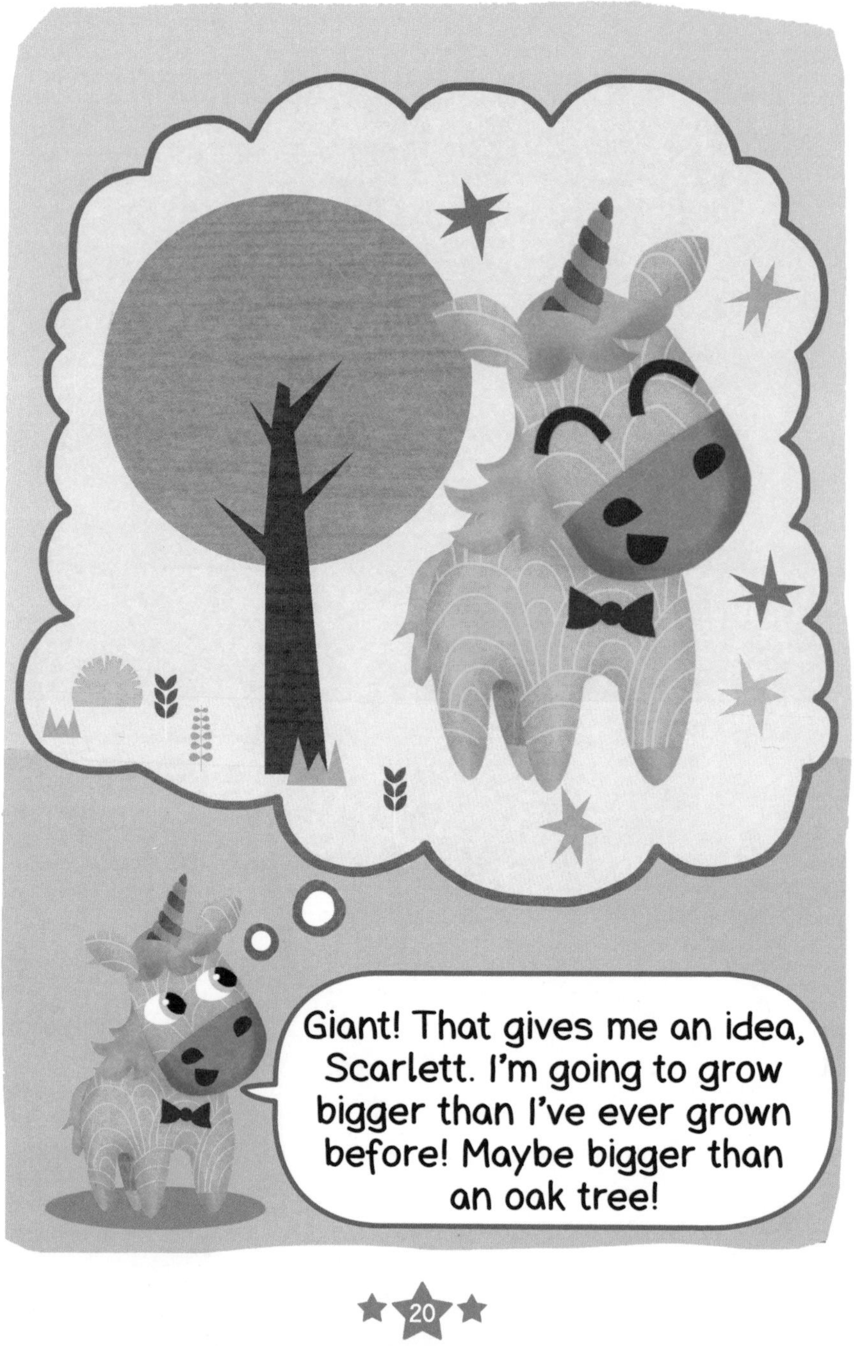
Giant! That gives me an idea, Scarlett. I'm going to grow bigger than I've ever grown before! Maybe bigger than an oak tree!

I have an idea! Lightning hit a tree in Budbloom Meadow and split it in two. Maybe I can use my healing powers to fix it!

Great ideas!

Everyone had **GLITTERY-GOOD** ideas. But by **CLOUDTIME**...

21

Sunny and I were still clueless.

Oooh, you're an amazing dancer, Bo! You could learn a dance that's so <u>twinkle</u>-<u>tastic</u> that a FULL-SIZE rainbow shoots from your hooves!

I love that idea! Thank you, Sunny!

Now I'm super excited to practice my new magic trick tomorrow. Nighty night, Diary!

3

What's Going On?!

Tuesday

We were practicing our magic tricks when suddenly –

Nutmeg fell from the sky, and she had hurt one of her hooves!

What happened?

I don't know! All of a sudden, I just couldn't fly anymore.

And ouch, my hoof hurts!

Don't worry, I'll heal it for you.

Piper swished her tail, but no sparkles appeared.

Hmmm. That's strange.

I could help!

Of course! I'll make a wish for my hoof to feel better.

Nutmeg made the wish. But again, no sparkles appeared!

26

Something strange is going on. Everyone, try to use your powers.

Scarlett couldn't magic anything from her mane. Jed couldn't change the weather. Sunny couldn't go invisible.

Then Monty sneezed and something horrible came out of his nose that definitely wasn't glitter.

ACHOO!

All our magic is GONE!

We wondered if Mr. Rumptwinkle had cast a spell on us as some sort of test. (He tricks us sometimes!) So we needed to talk to him.

Luckily, Nutmeg's hoof was feeling a bit better. So we trotted back to the unipods together to find Mr. Rumptwinkle.

On the way, we saw fairies who couldn't fly.

And we saw dragons who couldn't breathe fire.

It looks like the whole forest has lost its magic!

This can't be Mr. Rumptwinkle's doing, then.

But maybe he'll know how to fix it!

But Mr. Rumptwinkle had lost his powers, too! So he led us to Goblin Castle.

At the castle, there was a crowd of worried-looking creatures. Queen Juniper stood on her balcony.

If anyone will know what's going on, it'll be the queen.

Creatures of Sparklegrove Forest,
I, too, have lost my powers. But this
has never happened before,
so I don't know what to do.

Then an old gnome spoke up.

Sorry, Your Majesty. But you're wrong. This has happened before, and it was the work of a hobgoblin.

Some creatures gasped. Everyone knows hobgoblins haven't been seen in this forest for hundreds of years. Everyone was also shocked that the gnome had told the queen she was wrong!

The queen's guards stepped forward.

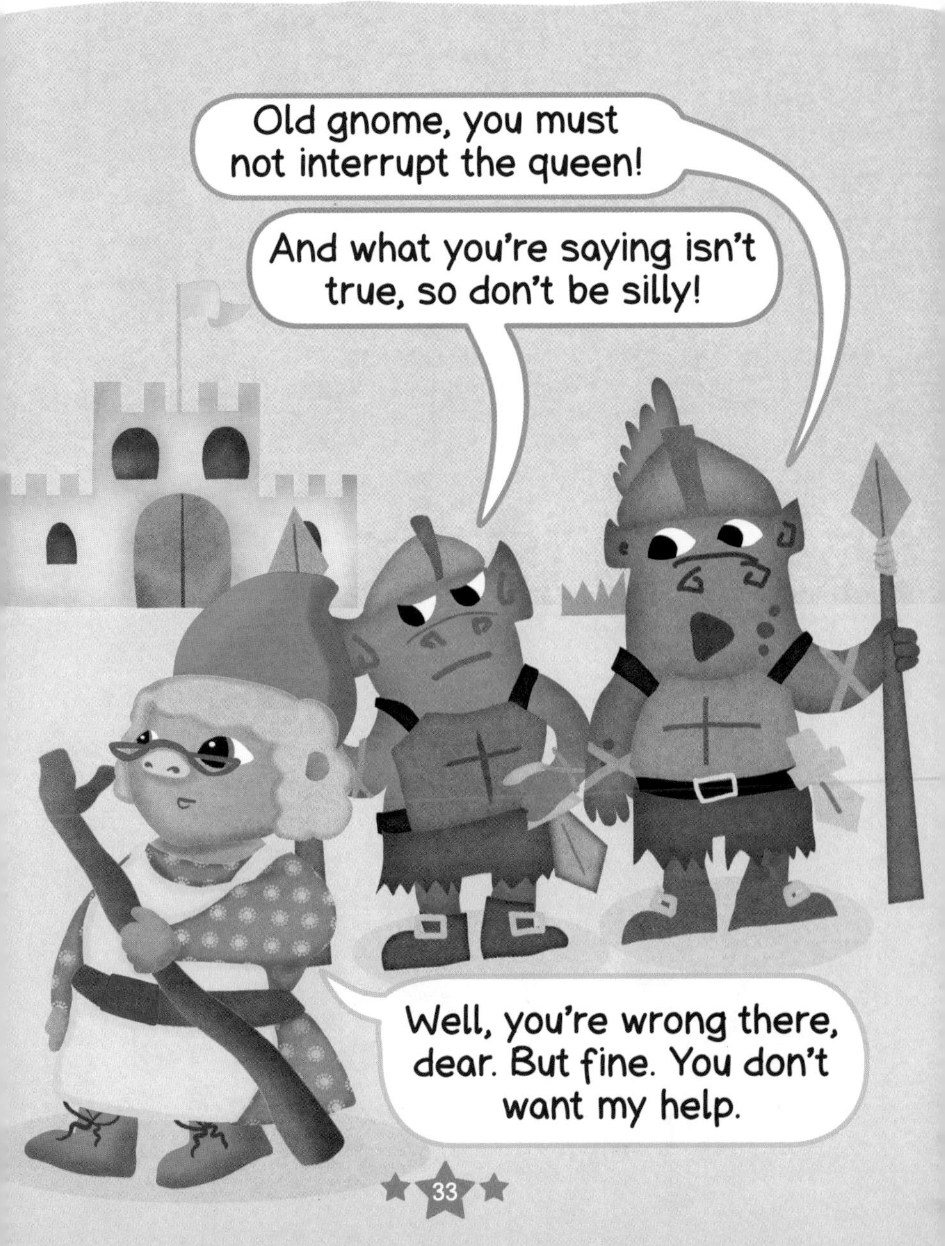

The gnome left, and Queen Juniper continued.

I will get to the bottom of the problem. But sadly, I have to cancel the Big Festival of Magic because . . . we have no magic. But keep calm and carry on.

At **CLOUDTIME**, our beds didn't float and our horns didn't glow.

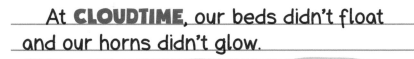

There must be something we can do!

That old gnome seemed to know something.

Maybe. But nobody's seen a hobgoblin in years!

True, but maybe we should hear the gnome's story?

We will find her in the morning. We must get the forest's magic back!

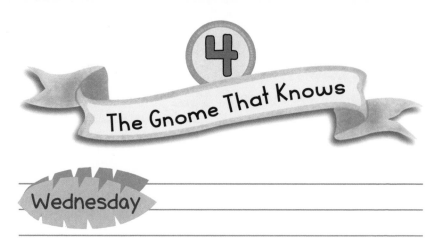

4

The Gnome That Knows

Wednesday

We woke up early and set off for the Gnome Tunnels.

When we got there, two gnomes were outside. They were helping a porcupine.

Hello! Where can we find the gnome who talked back to Queen Juniper yesterday?

Oh, that's Edna. Go underground. She's the third door on the left.

Thank you!

It was dark in the tunnels. I wished our horns could still glow! But we found Edna's door.

Hello, my dears! How can I help you?
Hello! Could you please tell us about the magic-stealing hobgoblin?
It's nice of you to ask. No one else wants to hear from me. They think I'm just old and silly.
We don't think that!
Well then, I'll make you dandelion syrup and tell you my story.

We sipped syrup as Edna
told us about the hobgoblins . . .

No one else remembers. But I'm the oldest gnome in the forest! I <u>know</u> this missing-magic business happened before! It was hundreds of years ago, when I was a young gnome.

There were two hobgoblins living in the forest then. One was my best friend! He was called Bob.

You were friends with a hobgoblin?
Yes, Bob was the best! But the other one was called Zagwart and he was evil.
Oooooh!

Edna continued her story.

Hobgoblins don't have magical powers. But they are very good at making special potions.

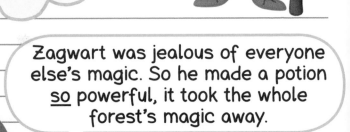

Zagwart was jealous of everyone else's magic. So he made a potion <u>so</u> powerful, it took the whole forest's magic away.

What happened next?

Eventually, Zagwart was forced to bring the magic back. And then he was chased out of the forest.

Hobgoblins have been banned from Sparklegrove Forest ever since.

But what about Bob?

Edna looked sad.

Nobody saw Bob after that. And I've missed my dear friend ever since. But because __all__ hobgoblins were banished, I guess I'll never see him again.

Poor Bob!

And poor you!

So, do you think Zagwart is back?

Well, yes. I can't think of another creature powerful and evil enough to steal our magic.

We all knew what we had to do: We had to find out if Zagwart was really back!

If Zagwart was here, where would he be?

He used to hide in a cave in Snowbelle Mountain. There's a secret entrance I can show you.

Edna packed syrup and cakes for our journey. Then we headed off.

Suddenly, a storm started up. We looked to Jed for help.

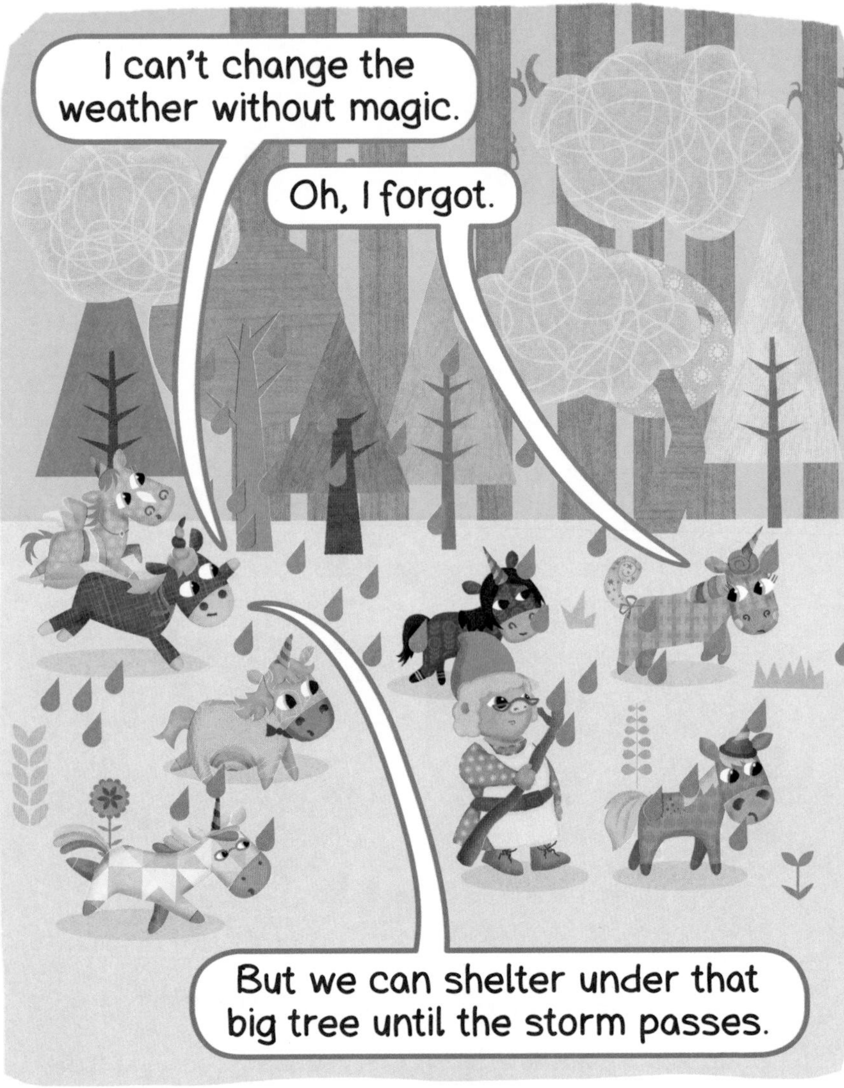
I can't change the weather without magic.
Oh, I forgot.
But we can shelter under that big tree until the storm passes.

We sheltered under the tree and ate some of Edna's cakes. Soon, fireflies fluttered around us. They ate our leftover crumbs!

We trotted along until we reached Snowbelle Mountain.

Edna showed us the secret entrance.

This is where Zagwart hid before!

That cave looks really dark.
And our horns can't glow.

Luckily, the fireflies followed us in so we could see.

We must be careful. If we find
Zagwart, we will just go tell the queen.

We were nervous, but we were super tired, too.

If Zagwart is here, he'll be hiding deep inside this mountain. So let's sleep here for the night and search more tomorrow.

We all felt a bit scared, but we eventually fell asleep . . .

5

The Hobgoblin

Thursday

We woke up early, still feeling a bit scared.

Come on! Now we need to be brave and find that hobgoblin!

We dropped cake crumbs for the fireflies as we trotted deeper into the mountain with Edna. The cave seemed to go on forever.

We've been in here for hours. I don't think Zagwart is here.

You're right. Maybe Edna had it wrong after all.

From the darkness, we heard a shaky voice.

Hello?

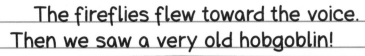
The fireflies flew toward the voice. Then we saw a very old hobgoblin!

Edna? Is that you?

AGH! Run! It's Zagwart!

No, it's not! It's . . . it's . . . Bob!

Oh, Edna, I've missed you!

Me too!

Edna and Bob were so happy to see each other after all this time! And Bob told us not to worry, as he was certain Zagwart never returned to the forest.

My goodness! How lovely it is to see you! No one has visited in such a long time! I'll make you <u>cloudberry</u> soup!

Bob did a little dance of joy as he made the soup!

We ate the soup fast. We were so hungry after giving most of our cakes away!

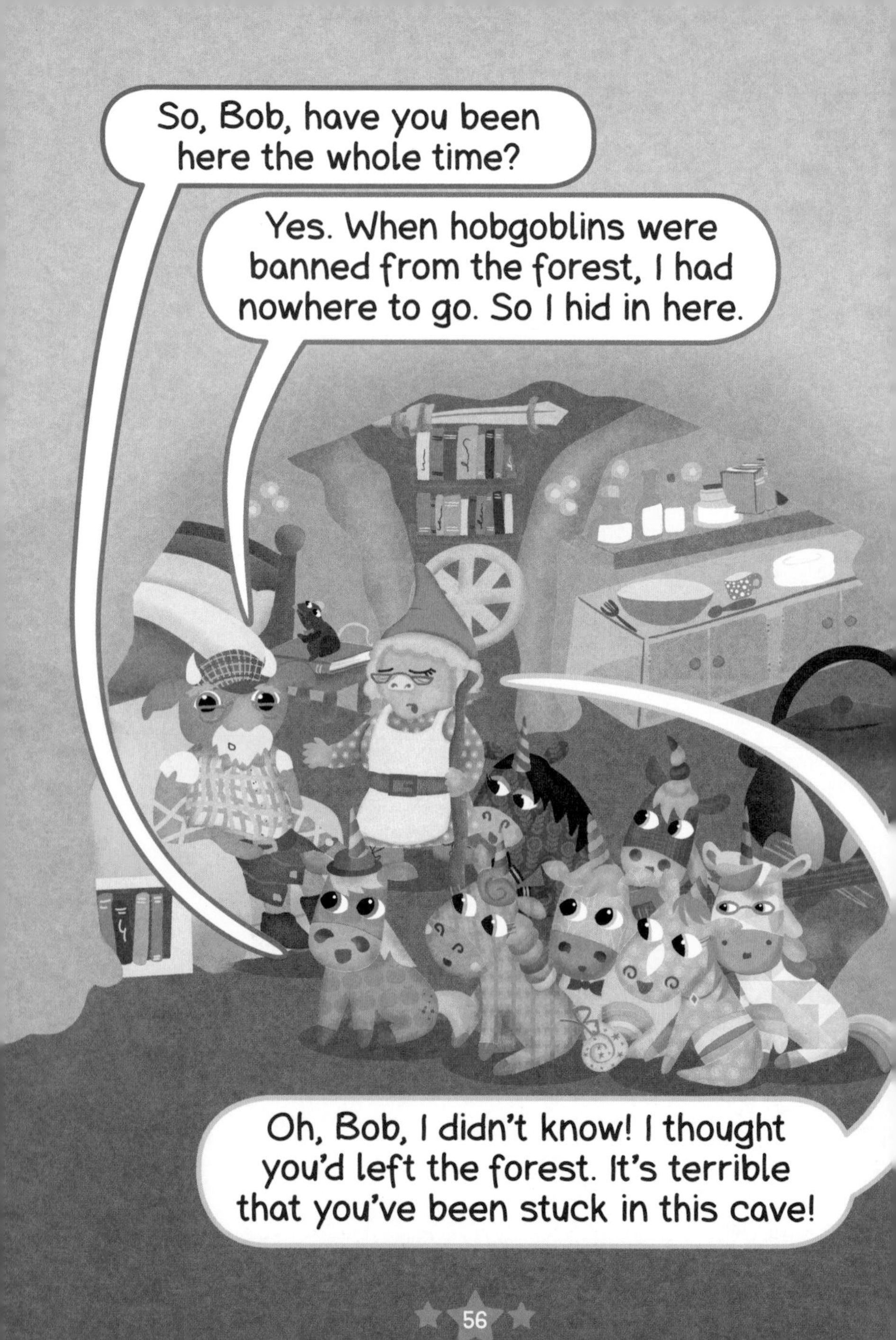
So, Bob, have you been here the whole time?
Yes. When hobgoblins were banned from the forest, I had nowhere to go. So I hid in here.
Oh, Bob, I didn't know! I thought you'd left the forest. It's terrible that you've been stuck in this cave!

It hasn't been so bad. I have my books!
And the fireflies keep me company.
I also have my pet rat, Scamper.
I did miss you though, Edna.

We felt so sorry Bob had been on his
own all this time. But it was **GLITTERRIFIC**
to see Edna and Bob reunited!

Now we still needed to find out what happened to the forest's magic.

Bob, we actually came looking for Zagwart because the forest has lost its magic again!

I know about that! Before Zagwart left, he made one last potion — to take away the forest's powers 500 years after he left.

We all looked at Bob with open
mouths as he looked at his watch.

Yup. It's been 500 years.

We were so excited to finally learn
what had happened. Next, we needed to
come up with a plan to get the magic back!

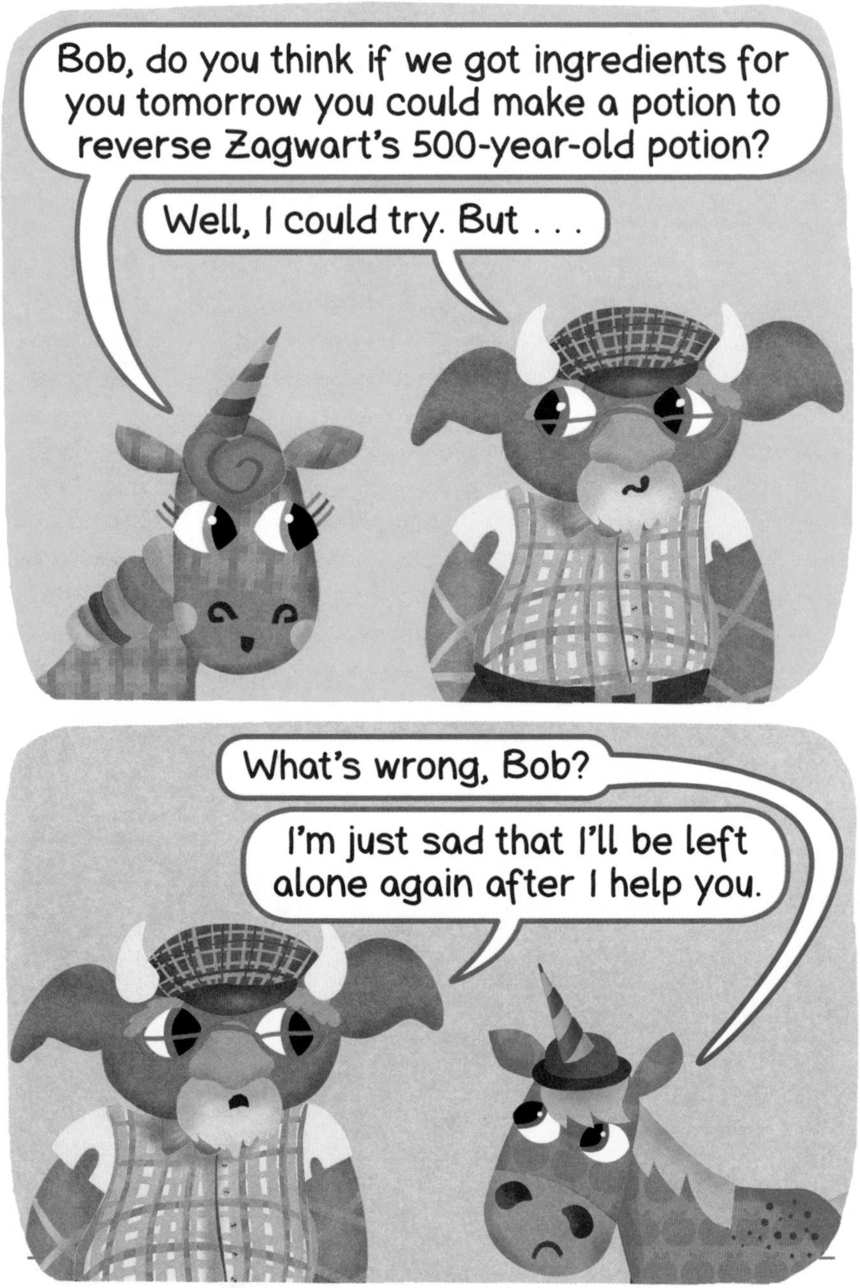
Bob, do you think if we got ingredients for you tomorrow you could make a potion to reverse Zagwart's 500-year-old potion?
Well, I could try. But . . .
What's wrong, Bob?
I'm just sad that I'll be left alone again after I help you.

If you bring the forest's magic back, I'm sure the queen will let you live in the forest again.

Yes, it's time to end the ban on hobgoblins!

Bob smiled. Soon, we all fell asleep as he and Edna told amazing stories from years ago.

6

The Magic Returns

We woke up ready to get the forest's magic back. Bob gave us a list of six ingredients for his special potion.

blueberries

the breath of a tree sprite

dandelions

elderflowers

the left sock of a yeti

thistles

We collected everything.

Thank you!

Bob mixed the potion. But then he said he needed one more thing . . .

We need a special <u>secret</u> ingredient. It can be very hard to find, but I think you've all found it in one another.

What do you mean?

Hold hooves and stand in a circle around the cauldron. If I'm right, this should make the potion work.

Soon, swirls of sparkles exploded from the cauldron! We felt our powers come back right away!

Yay! Your potion worked!

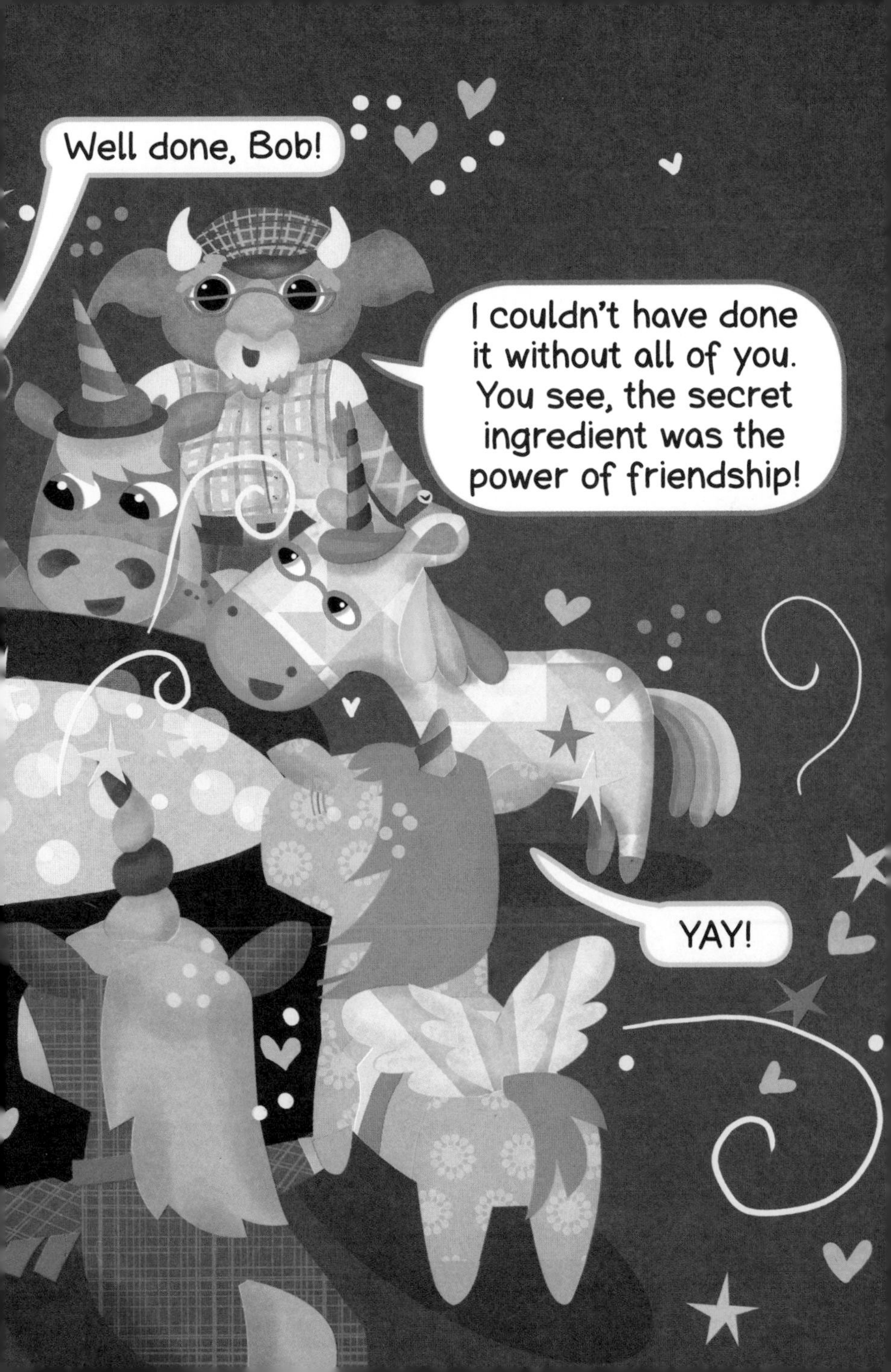
Well done, Bob!
I couldn't have done it without all of you. You see, the secret ingredient was the power of friendship!
YAY!

We trotted to Goblin Castle to tell Queen Juniper the good news — that the magic was back! At first, she didn't believe us. So we suggested she try to fly.

But then she saw Bob and screamed!

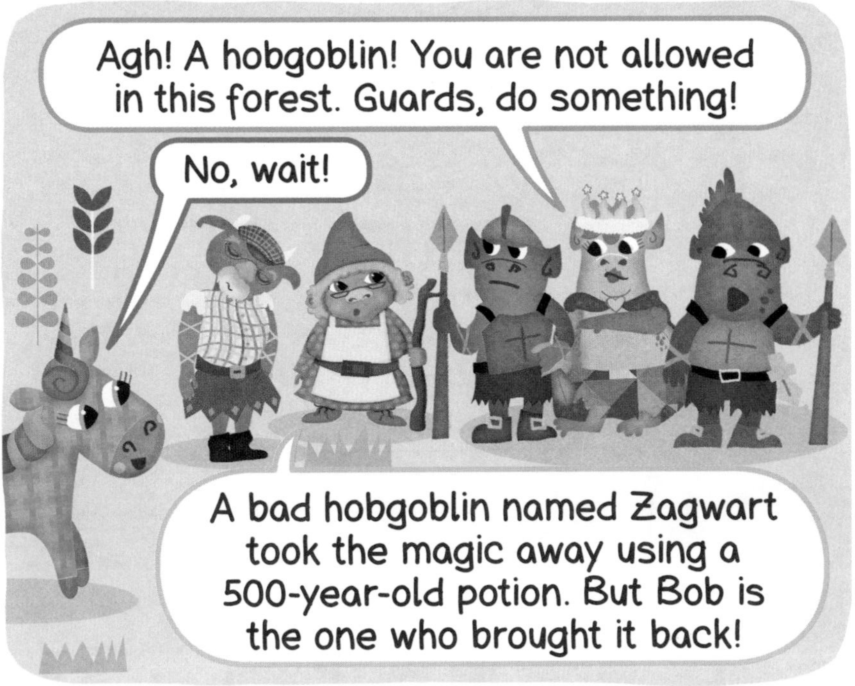
Agh! A hobgoblin! You are not allowed in this forest. Guards, do something!
No, wait!
A bad hobgoblin named Zagwart took the magic away using a 500-year-old potion. But Bob is the one who brought it back!

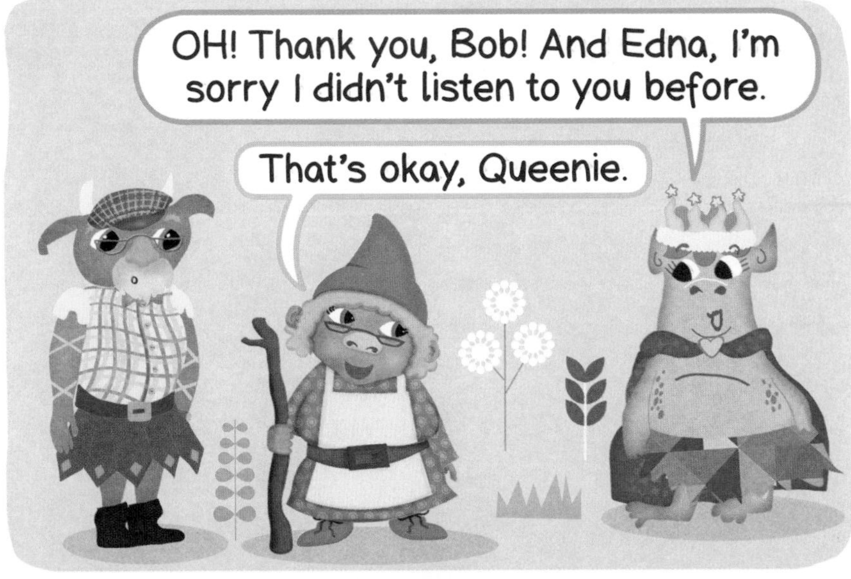
OH! Thank you, Bob! And Edna, I'm sorry I didn't listen to you before.
That's okay, Queenie.

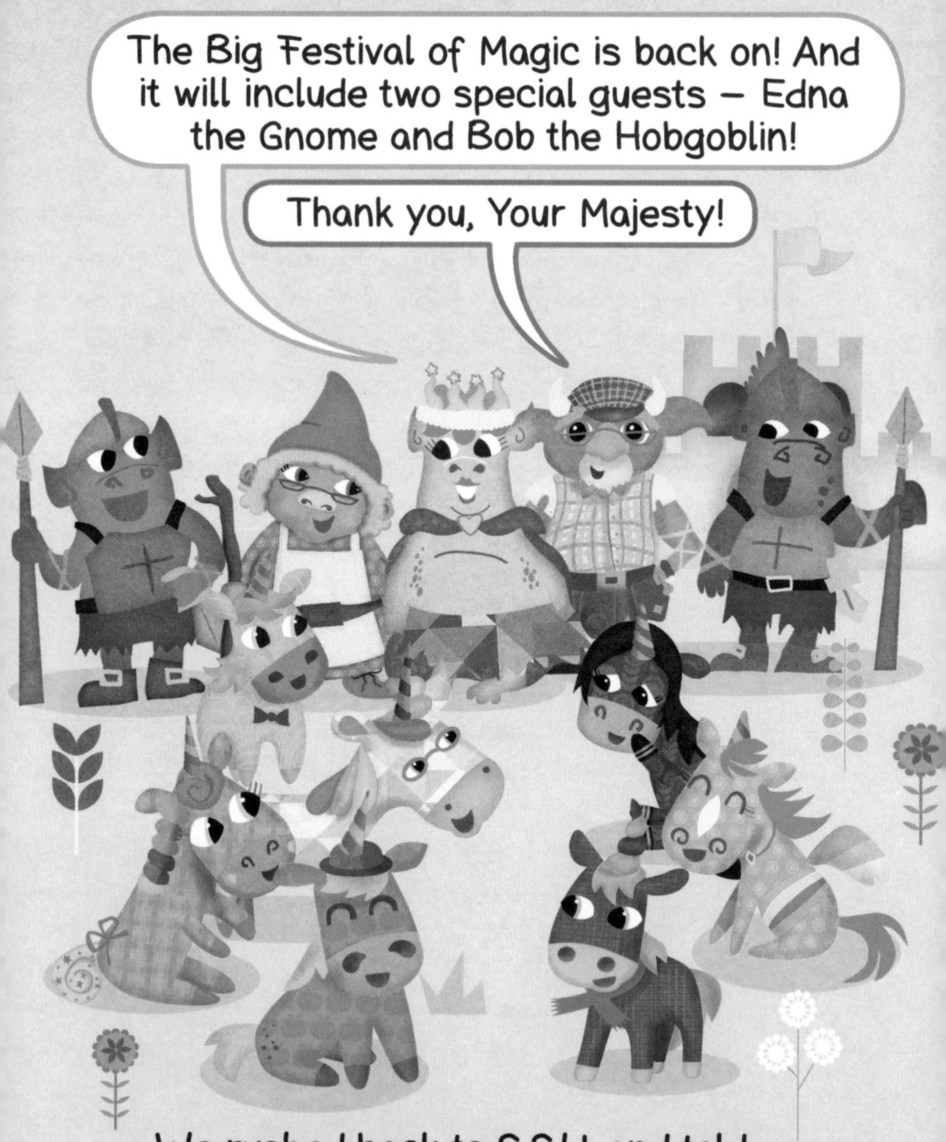
The Big Festival of Magic is back on! And it will include two special guests – Edna the Gnome and Bob the Hobgoblin!
Thank you, Your Majesty!

We rushed back to S.S.U. and told Mr. Rumptwinkle about our adventure and the good news about tomorrow's festival.

Unicorns, I am so proud of you! You will definitely get your MAGIC patches tomorrow!

But how have we earned them? We've hardly used our magic!

That's just it. The way you worked TOGETHER to solve a very big problem was more magical than magic itself!

We spent the rest of the day practicing our magic tricks for the festival. Tomorrow's going to be so much fun!

7
A Magical Day

Saturday

The festival was **SPARKLE-TASTIC**! Queen Juniper gave Bob and Edna awards for SPECIAL SERVICES TO MAGIC. Dragons made fireworks, mermaids did water ballet, trolls juggled rocks, and fairies jousted!

Us unicorns were super nervous to perform our magic tricks. But we did well! And the crowd cheered when we earned our patches!

(Oh, and they laughed when Sunny's bottom ran around on its own!)

We danced the night away under the GIANT rainbow that I magicked from my hooves!

What a busy week, Diary! We went on an adventure, made two friends, and learned new skills. Best of all, we learned that even without actual magic, life is truly magical. See you next time!

Rebecca Elliott may not have a magical horn or sneeze glitter, but she's still a lot like a unicorn. Rebecca always tries to have a positive attitude, she likes to laugh a lot, and she lives with some great creatures — her noisy-yet-charming children, her lovable but naughty dog, Frida, and a big, lazy cat named Bernard. She gets to hang out with these fun characters and write stories for a living, so she thinks her life is pretty magical!

Rebecca is the author of several picture books, the young adult novel PRETTY FUNNY FOR A GIRL, the bestselling Unicorn Diaries early chapter book series, and the bestselling Owl Diaries series.

Unicorn Diaries

How much do you know about The Missing Magic?

Why doesn't anyone listen to Edna when Edna first says magic went missing before? Reread pages 32 and 33.

Why were hobgoblins banished from Sparklegrove Forest? Do you think it was right to make Bob leave when only Zagwart caused trouble?

Bob did not see his friend Edna for many years. Think about when you went a long time without seeing a friend. How did you feel when you saw them again?

The unicorns are working to earn their MAGIC patches. How do they earn them?

List the new ways each unicorn uses their magic. Draw your favorite unicorns doing their tricks!

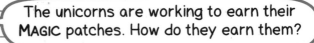